11/15

Fairy Tales

A Treasury

LITTLE, BROWN & COMPANY

LB kids

Little, Brown and Company

Hachette Book Group
1290 Avenue of the Americas, New York, NY 10104
Visit us at lb-kids.com

LB kids is an imprint of Little, Brown and Company.
The LB kids name and logo are trademarks of Hachette Book Group, Inc.

The publisher is not responsible for websites (or their content)
that are not owned by the publisher.

First Edition: October 2015

Library of Congress Control Number: 2015938649

ISBN 978-0-316-37856-7

10 9 8 7 6 5 4 3 2 1

APS

Printed in China

Table of Contents

Welcome to Pixie Hollow 5

Tinker Bell and the Lost Treasure 53

Tinker Bell and the Great Fairy Rescue 99

Tinker Bell and the Secret of the Wings 147

Tinker Bell and the Pirate Fairy 185

Tinker Bell and the Legend of the NeverBeast 225

Welcome to Pixie Hollow

Year after year, the seasons come and go, bringing with them enchanting changes. Snowflakes melt to reveal spring's hopeful shoots of green. Summer flowers bloom until it is time for autumn's leaves to fill the world with color. It may appear to be magic, but in fact, these transformations are the work of fairies.

Every fairy starts out as a baby's first laugh. On one winter's day in London, a baby laughed for the first time, and that laugh floated up and away to meet its destiny.

The laugh floated toward
an island, picking up speed as it
neared a magical place in the heart
of Never Land, where anything was
possible. This was Pixie Hollow,
home of the fabulous fairies!

"Come on! Let's go!" the fairies
cried, following the newcomer.

Vidia, the fastest-flying fairy,
used her speed to guide the delicate
wisp into the branches of the Pixie
Dust Tree.

A dust-keeper fairy named Terence came forward and sprinkled the wisp with pixie dust. It flickered and let out a tinkling sound, then took the shape of a tiny, adorable fairy.

The other fairies welcomed her as she gazed at her surroundings with wonder.

The new fairy looked up as Queen Clarion approached.

"Born of laughter, clothed in cheer, happiness has brought you here. Welcome to Pixie Hollow," said the queen.

Then she helped the fairy unfurl her wings.

Next, Queen Clarion waved her hand, and several toadstools sprang up around the Pixie Dust Well. Fairies began to flitter forward, placing different objects on the pedestals.

Rosetta, a garden fairy, brought a flower. Silvermist, a water fairy, carried a droplet of water. Iridessa, a light fairy, placed a glowing lamp on her pedestal.

"They will help you find your talent," the queen explained.

The new fairy placed her hand on the beautiful flower. Its glow instantly faded. She reached for the water droplet, but that, too, faded. And then when she touched the lamp, it lost its glow. What could her talent be?

The fairy moved on without touching anything else—she was afraid to fail again.

But, as she passed a hammer, it began to glow. Then it rose up off its pedestal and flew straight into her delicate hands!

"I've never seen one glow that much before," said Silvermist.

"I do believe you're right," agreed Rosetta.

Queen Clarion was pleased. The newcomer was a tinker-talent fairy.

Queen Clarion called upon the tinker fairies of Pixie Hollow.

"Please welcome the newest member of your talent guild," the queen announced. "Her name is Tinker Bell!"

The tinker fairies rushed forward.

"We're pleased as a pile of perfectly polished pots you're here," said Bobble, who wore dewdrop glasses.

And with that, the tinkers whisked Tinker Bell off for a flying tour of Pixie Hollow.

"Welcome to Tinkers' Nook!" said Bobble as
the trio headed in for a landing.

Tinker Bell looked down to find a charming little
courtyard lined with twig-and-leaf cottages. Tink loved
the bustle of activity as fairies fixed and fashioned all
kinds of amazing useful objects.

Clank and Bobble finished their tour by showing
Tinker Bell the houses where the tinker fairies lived.

The last stop was Tinker Bell's new home, nestled in a mossy knothole.

"We were hoping the new arrival would be one of us, so we got the place all ready," Bobble explained.

The friendly pair left Tinker Bell to put on the work clothes they had found for her. The garments turned out to be much too big, but Tink knew just how to fix them!

Tinker Bell put on her new dress and tied up her hair. Then she reported to the tinker workshop. Clank and Bobble couldn't wait to show her all the handy things that tinker fairies make.

Soon, Fairy Mary, who runs Tinkers' Nook, arrived.

"Ah! A new tinker fairy," Fairy Mary said, greeting Tinker Bell. "So dainty! Don't worry, dear, we'll build up those tinker muscles in no time."

Then, after reminding Clank and Bobble to make their deliveries, Fairy Mary was gone.

Clank, Bobble, and Tinker Bell left for the meadow. Cheese the mouse helped them pull their wagon.

When they arrived, Bobble invited the fairies to gather around. "We've brought some new spring items!" he said.

There were rainbow light tubes for Iridessa, milkweed pods for Fawn, and pussy-willow brushes for Rosetta.

"What are you going to do with those?" Tink asked.

Iridessa explained they would take them to the Mainland to change the seasons—but only nature-talent fairies traveled there.

Tinker Bell returned to the workshop, where
Fairy Mary was organizing supplies.

"Being a tinker stinks," Tink grumbled to herself.

"Excuse me?" replied Fairy Mary.

"Why don't we get to go to the Mainland?" Tink asked.

"The day you can magically make the flowers grow, or
capture the rays of the sun or whatnot, then you can go.
Until then, your work is here," said Fairy Mary.

Suddenly, Tink smiled. "Good idea!" she said.

The next morning, Tinker Bell caught up with her friends at the Pixie Dust Well.

"If you could teach me your talents," she said, "maybe the queen would let me go to the Mainland for spring."

"I've never heard of someone switching talents," Iridessa said.

"You all do things that are beautiful, and magical, and important," Tink said. "But there's got to be more to my life than just pots and kettles. All I'm asking is that you give me a chance."

"There's a first time for everything, I guess," declared Rosetta. "What harm can come from trying?"

Tink's first lesson was how to become a
water-talent fairy. Silvermist showed her how
to lift a dewdrop and place it on a spider's web.

Tink tried again and again. Each time, the
dewdrop burst before she could even carry it
over to the web.

"Maybe you're a light-talent fairy,"
Silvermist said.

That evening, it was Iridessa's turn to give Tink a lesson. Iridessa captured some sunset light in a bucket, then scattered a handful into the air. Dozens of fireflies flew through the glow and lit up their bottoms.

Tink tried to copy Iridessa, but the light wouldn't stick to her fingers. Now she was glowing, too—and the fireflies thought she was the most beautiful thing they had ever seen!

Fawn had Tink's animal-fairy lesson all planned. "We're teaching baby birds how to fly," she announced.

Fawn showed Tink exactly what to do. She went over to a baby and gently encouraged it until the fluffy little creature was flying along behind her.

Unfortunately, Tink's baby bird seemed terrified. Tink had no luck as an animal-talent fairy, either.

A little while later, Tinker Bell flew to the beach. "At this rate, I should get to the Mainland right about— oh, never!"

She threw a pebble and heard a CLUNK! Tink went to investigate and found a wonderful surprise: a beautiful porcelain box.

Tinker Bell lifted the lid. "Wow!" she sighed, seeing the springs and gears inside. There were more parts lying in the dirt. She gathered them up and set to work.

By the time her friends found her, Tinker Bell was elbow-deep in the box. The girls watched, unseen, as their friend put the trinket back together. They were amazed.

Tink spotted one more part sticking out of the underbrush. It was a brass post with a porcelain ballerina. Tink fitted the post into the lid and gave the dancer a spin. To her delight, the box played music!

Tink's friends came out of their hiding places to admire her beautiful work.

"Do you even realize what you're doing?" asked Rosetta. "Creating those gadgets, figuring things out, fixing stuff like this— that's what tinkering is!"

Tink did love tinkering. But she wanted to go to the Mainland more than anything, and tinkering wasn't going to get her there.

That night, Queen Clarion called an emergency meeting. The spring preparations were wrecked in an accident. They were going to need to get ready all over again!

"I don't think we can fix this in time," said the minister of spring. "We're going to have to cancel spring, or postpone it at the very least."

The ministers of winter, summer, and autumn all started to panic.

"Settle down," pleaded the queen. "Fairy Mary, is it even possible to redo everything in such a short time?"

Fairy Mary used her abacus. "No," she said.

When news got around to the fairies, Tinker
Bell had an idea!

"Hello, Miss Bell!" said Clank and Bobble.
"Can we help you with something?"

Tinker Bell explained that they needed to save
spring! "Gather up all the twigs you can...and tree
sap. But most importantly, we need to find lots of
trinkets," Tinker Bell said.

Everyone flew off in different directions. They
brought Tink whatever they could find, and soon
the square was filled with piles of useful objects.

Tink showed a group of fairies how to assemble a machine to make berry paint.

Next, Tink rigged up some more paint sprayers and set Fawn and Silvermist to work on the ladybugs.

Fawn sprayed on the red and then sent them over to Silvermist to put on the black dots.

Tink stood over a collection of knickknacks and lost things, wondering what she could make with them. Suddenly, she put together a vacuum using a glove and a harmonica. It would collect huge amounts of seeds at a time.

Everywhere she looked, Tinker Bell could see rows and piles and baskets and buckets of springtime supplies—and more on the way.

"It's working!" shouted Iridessa.

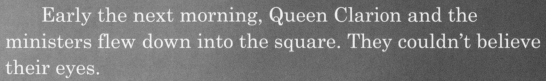

Early the next morning, Queen Clarion and the ministers flew down into the square. They couldn't believe their eyes.

An Everblossom opened and gave off a golden glow, signaling that it was time to bring springtime to the world.

The fairies of Pixie Hollow cheered.

"You did it, Tinker Bell," said Queen Clarion.

"We all did it," Tink replied.

Suddenly, Clank and Bobble pulled in a wagon. Tink's music box was inside, all polished and shiny.

"Surprise!" Clank and Bobble shouted.

"I actually ran across this myself many seasons ago," said Fairy Mary. "I didn't have a clue what it was, but you did, Tinker Bell. I'd imagine there's someone out there who's missing this. Perhaps a certain tinker fairy has a job to do on the Mainland."

Tink couldn't believe it. She would be going to the Mainland after all!

The magical fairies spread across the Mainland and got straight to work! A light fairy melted the frost on a tree branch. A water fairy cast the sparkle of pixie dust on a pond.

Little by little, the world was filled with color, light, and life. Flowers bloomed. A dazzling rainbow reached across the sky. Baby birds took flight.

Tinker Bell watched in amazement as her new friends brought beauty to the world. But most importantly, Tinker Bell was proud to be a tinker fairy!

The End

Tinker Bell and the Lost Treasure

Fairies took to the sky above Pixie Hollow. It was time to bring the beautiful season of autumn to the Mainland!

Unseen by the humans below, they burst through the clouds and began working their magic. The leaves on the trees turned brilliant shades of red, orange, and gold.

Animals were prepared for the colder months ahead. Glorious pumpkins and crisp apples ripened and were ready for harvest.

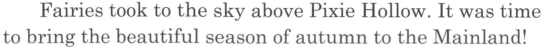

Back in Pixie Hollow, other fairies were busily collecting and delivering pixie dust from the Pixie Dust Tree. It was this pixie dust that allowed the fairies to change the seasons—and made it possible for all fairies to do their magic.

"Come on, let's go, flap your wings," said Fairy Gary, the leader of the Pixie Dust Depot.

Soon the buzzer signaling the end of the workday sounded, and Terence eagerly headed out to help his best friend, Tinker Bell, with her latest invention.

But Terence was unable to find Tinker Bell because at that same moment Tinker Bell was requested to see Queen Clarion right away! A summoning fairy named Viola brought her to the queen.

The minister of autumn revealed the real
reason they had summoned her.

"For some time now," the minister
began, "fairies have celebrated the end of
autumn with a revelry—and this particular autumn coincides
with a Blue Harvest Moon. A new scepter must be created to
celebrate the occasion."

He led Tinker Bell to a pair of heavy oak doors and pushed them
open. Tinker Bell stared in awe at a dazzling display of ornate scepters.

"Every scepter is unique," explained the minister. "Some are
the work of animal fairies, while others are the work of light fairies
or garden fairies. This year, it is the turn of the tinker fairies."

"And Fairy Mary has recommended *you*," Queen Clarion
declared.

Tinker Bell gasped in disbelief. "But...but I'm..."

"A very talented tinker," Fairy Mary finished.

"The scepter must be built to precise dimensions," the minister said emphatically. "At the top, you will place a moonstone." He directed everyone's attention to a picture hanging on the wall. "When the Blue Moon is at its peak, its rays will pass through the gem, creating Blue Pixie Dust. This Blue Dust restores the Pixie Dust Tree. We are relying on you."

Tinker Bell got to work right away. She tried many different designs for the scepter. Terence joined her day after day because he knew a lot about the Blue Moon and moonstone.

"The Blue Moon only rises in Pixie Hollow every eight years," Terence said. "The path of the light beams must match the shape of the moonstone at a ninety-degree angle so the light can transform the pixie dust."

Tinker Bell was impressed that he knew so much about the gem.

"Remember, you get the most Blue Pixie Dust if you maximize the moonstone's surface area," Terence reminded.

"Right. Got it," replied Tink gratefully.

She couldn't have asked for a more helpful assistant.

But later that day, after running out for supplies, Terence proudly rolled in a compass he had found at the cove.

Tinker Bell accidentally bumped the compass with her hip, and it rolled across the room.

WHACK!

The compass hit the scepter, which tripped Terence, and the moonstone fell from his hands and broke into pieces.

"My scepter!" Tink cried.

That night, Tink tried to glue the moonstone back together.
Just as it fell apart again, Clank and Bobble stopped by. Tinker
Bell panicked and swept the moonstone fragments into a bag.

"We came to see if you wanted to join us at the Fairy-Tale
Theater," said Clank.

"Look, guys, I really don't have time," Tink answered.

But before they went on their way, Bobble told Tink that
Fairy Mary would be there. Suddenly, Tinker Bell realized
that Fairy Mary might know how to find another moonstone.

"Wait for me!" she called after them.

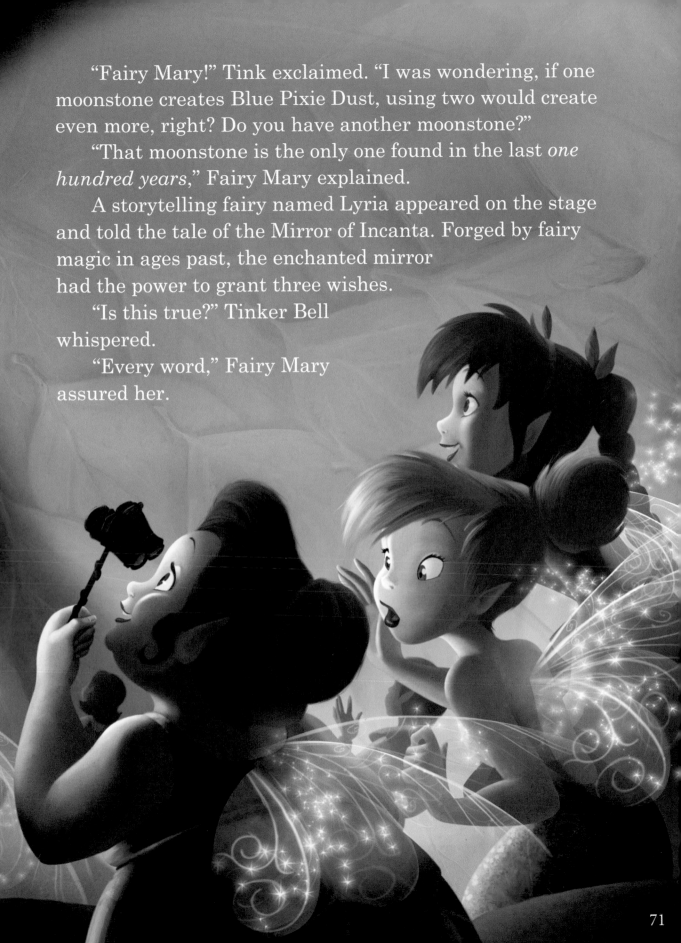

"Fairy Mary!" Tink exclaimed. "I was wondering, if one moonstone creates Blue Pixie Dust, using two would create even more, right? Do you have another moonstone?"

"That moonstone is the only one found in the last *one hundred years*," Fairy Mary explained.

A storytelling fairy named Lyria appeared on the stage and told the tale of the Mirror of Incanta. Forged by fairy magic in ages past, the enchanted mirror had the power to grant three wishes.

"Is this true?" Tinker Bell whispered.

"Every word," Fairy Mary assured her.

Pretending to be tired, Tink left the theater as quickly as she could. She had to find that mirror and wish to restore the moonstone!

Back at home, Tink quickly drew a map of the Lost Island, consulted the compass, and began to pack some supplies.

"How am I going to carry all this?" she wondered as she checked her bag of pixie dust. "This does not look like enough."

But Tink wasn't too worried.

Despite not knowing if she had enough pixie
dust for her journey, Tinker Bell moved ahead
with her plan to design and build a vehicle that
could carry her and all her supplies to the Lost
Island. She used a gourd boat, a bunch of cotton
balls, and an array of pots and pans.

At dusk, Tink sprinkled the balloon with
pixie dust and lifted off with the broken
moonstone safely tucked in her satchel.

"So long, Pixie Hollow," Tinker Bell called as
she rose higher and higher into the sky. "I'll be
back soon."

According to Tink's map, it wouldn't be long until she reached her destination.

"Whew, I'm starving," she suddenly realized. Tink opened one of her supply bags and found—nothing but crumbs! Then she reached into her other bag and was met with a low growl. She cautiously looked inside and discovered an adorable little firefly with a very full tummy.

"My cheese! My pumpernickel muffins!" Tink cried.

The little bug perked up and made it clear that he wanted to help, but Tink was determined to find the mirror on her own.

Tinker Bell turned her attention back to her map. But it was so dark, she couldn't see a thing!

Then, suddenly, the map was illuminated by a gentle glow. It was the little firefly!

"Oh, all right," Tink said, giving in. "You can stay. For now. I'm Tinker Bell. What's your name?" The insect glowed brighter. "Blinky? Flicker? Flash? Beam? Flare?" Tink guessed. Then it came to her. "Oh, Blaze."

Meanwhile, everyone in Pixie Hollow was hard at work preparing for the revelry. Cheese the mouse helped Iridessa hang lanterns, while Silvermist taught pollywogs how to blow festive bubbles. Fawn and Rosetta helped, too.

Fairy Mary was pleased with their progress. There was nothing she liked more than to see the fairies bustling with efficiency—especially with an event as important as the Autumn Revelry coming up!

Finally, after landing the balloon, Tink
and Blaze were guided through the forest
and to a cliff by some new bug friends.
There, in the distance, was the stone arch.

"Thank you all so much," she told the
little creatures. "Great to have friends that'll
help you out, huh?" Tink said to Blaze.

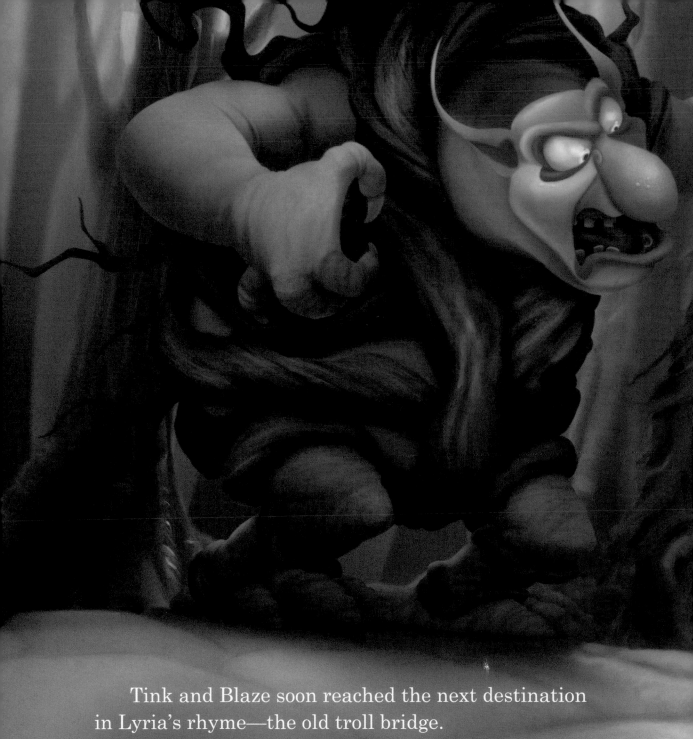

Tink and Blaze soon reached the next destination in Lyria's rhyme—the old troll bridge.

But the trolls weren't cooperating. "Beat it before we grind your bones to make our bed," said the small troll.

"Make our 'bread,'" corrected the tall troll. Soon the two were having a heated argument.

They were so busy squabbling that they didn't even notice when Tink and Blaze tiptoed over the bridge!

Tink and Blaze continued across the island. Finally, they emerged from the brush onto a beautiful beach. Tink was overjoyed. From there, she could see the pirates' shipwreck that Lyria had talked about!

"'The ship that sunk but never sank,'" Tinker Bell quoted. "Okay, Blaze, this is it! We've got to find that mirror and fix the moonstone. Let's go!"

Inside the shipwreck, Blaze shined his light on a treasure pile, and something shined back.

Tink reached into the treasure and pulled out the mirror!

"It's real," she said, not quite believing it.

Tink laid the fragments of the moonstone in front of the mirror and then took a deep breath.

"I wish…" she began but was distracted by Blaze buzzing near her ear.

"Blaze, I wish you'd be quiet for one minute!" Tinker Bell exploded.

Blaze's buzzing stopped.

Tinker Bell gasped. "That wasn't my wish! Blaze, look what you've done!"

Right away, Tink felt bad. "I'm sorry. It's not your fault, Blaze. It's mine," she admitted.

"I just wish Terence were here," Tinker Bell cried. Suddenly, Terence's face appeared in the mirror.

"Terence!" Tinker Bell exclaimed.

"I am with you," said Terence. He was standing right behind her! He had known she might need help.

Tink and Terence collected the mirror and a few more treasures and headed back to the balloon.

Terence used some of his pixie dust to help the balloon fly.

"I don't know if it will help, but I brought this," said Terence. He handed Tink the shattered scepter.

Together, they worked through the night to repair the broken scepter as the Blue Moon rose higher in the sky.

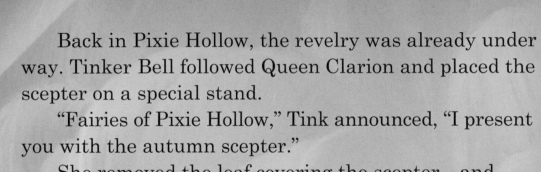

Back in Pixie Hollow, the revelry was already under way. Tinker Bell followed Queen Clarion and placed the scepter on a special stand.

"Fairies of Pixie Hollow," Tink announced, "I present you with the autumn scepter."

She removed the leaf covering the scepter—and everyone gasped! This scepter was nothing like the orderly creations of the past.

WHOOSH!

The moonbeams reflected everywhere and streaked above the crowd, raining down the rare Blue Pixie Dust.

At first a flurry, then a dust fall, then a blizzard, the dust swirled in the air before settling in drifts on the ground.

"Your Majesty!" the minister of autumn cried jubilantly. "I've never seen this much Blue Pixie Dust before!"

Silvermist, Fawn, Iridessa, and Rosetta were amazed. "Only Tinker Bell," Iridessa said affectionately.

"Fairies of Pixie Hollow," Queen Clarion said, "we have celebrated this revelry without interruption for centuries. Tonight, I believe, is our finest revelry ever, thanks to one very special fairy—Tinker Bell.

"And her friend Terence," the queen added. "And her new friend, Blaze."

All the fairies cheered. "I'm so proud of you," Fairy Mary told Tink.

The minister of autumn handed Tink the scepter. "All right, everyone, to the Pixie Dust Tree," he announced as Tinker Bell led the procession.

The End

Tinker Bell and the Great Fairy Rescue

Tinker Bell and her fairy friends were on their way to bring summer to the Mainland—and Tink couldn't wait to get there!

Summer needed the fairies' constant attention—which meant that Tink was going to be on the Mainland for months instead of days. Tinker Bell was so excited! She had heard so many amazing stories about the fairy camp where they'd be staying.

Once they arrived on the Mainland, the nature fairies instantly got to work.

Vidia, a fast-flying fairy, created a breeze that made the summer grasses sway softly.

Iridessa, a light fairy, bathed flowers in sunshine.

Fawn, an animal fairy, warmly greeted some birds, while Silvermist, a water fairy, frolicked with playful pollywogs.

Rosetta, a garden fairy, helped bees find their way to the flowers' sweet nectar.

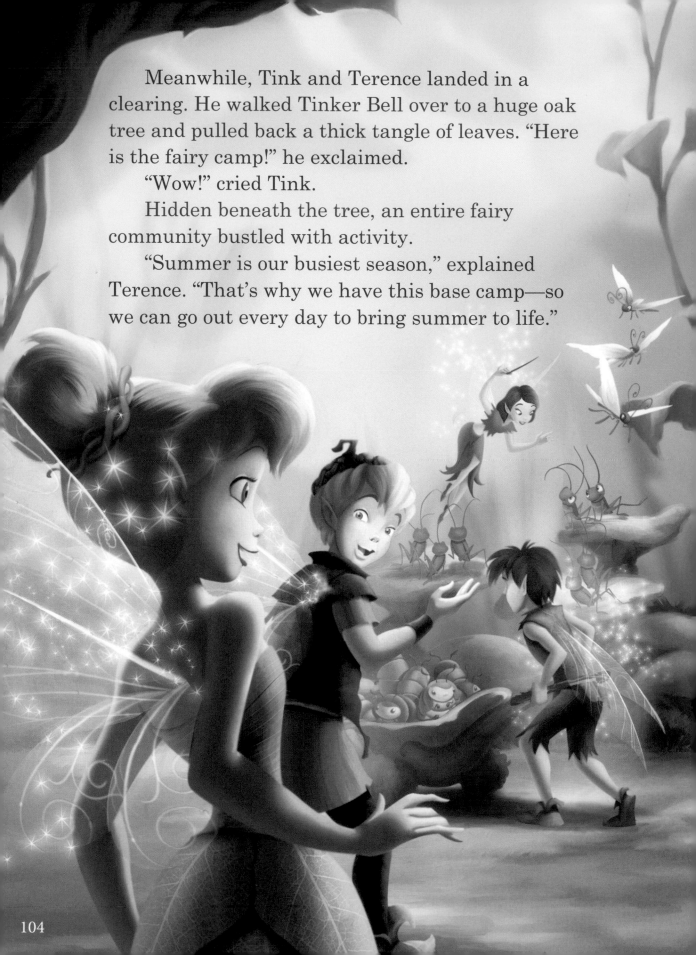

Meanwhile, Tink and Terence landed in a clearing. He walked Tinker Bell over to a huge oak tree and pulled back a thick tangle of leaves. "Here is the fairy camp!" he exclaimed.

"Wow!" cried Tink.

Hidden beneath the tree, an entire fairy community bustled with activity.

"Summer is our busiest season," explained Terence. "That's why we have this base camp—so we can go out every day to bring summer to life."

Tink couldn't wait to start tinkering!
She went to talk to a couple of animal fairies
painting stripes and patterns on butterflies.

Just then, a loud CRACK! traveled
through the fairy camp!

Fawn knocked over some paint, and the
splattered butterfly took off. The loud noise
made Tinker Bell very curious.

The other fairies hid, but Tinker Bell went to see where the noise had come from. She was intrigued by the sight of an automobile making its way down the winding road—and took off after it!

"Tinker Bell!" Vidia cried. She couldn't believe Tink would do something so dangerous! But she followed her anyway.

The car was carrying the Griffiths family—
eight-year-old Lizzy; her father, Dr. Griffiths; and
their cat, Mr. Twitches.

Tink followed the automobile until it stopped at
an old house in the country.

"Could we have a tea party in the meadow? Could
we? Please, please, please?" Lizzy pleaded as her
father unloaded their suitcases.

Dr. Griffiths looked at her wearily. "Not today,"
he said. "I have quite a bit of work to do. Perhaps
tomorrow."

Tink and Vidia waited until the humans were
in the house and flew over to examine the car.

Just then, Lizzy and her father returned to finish unloading the car.

Tink and Vidia froze, but the humans' attention was focused on a butterfly.

"The wings have two entirely different patterns," Dr. Griffiths observed.

"Well, I guess that's just the way the fairies decided to paint it," Lizzy said.

Her father was quick to correct her.

"Fairies do not paint butterfly wings, because, as you know, fairies are not real," he declared as he pushed the butterfly into a net.

Tinker Bell and Vidia snuck out from under the car and explored the area around the Griffiths' house.

Tink landed next to a row of buttons lined up like stepping-stones. "These will be perfect for the new wagon prototype I've been working on."

"I'm not carrying this human junk back to camp...." began Vidia, but then she stopped in awe. In front of her was Lizzy's fairy house.

"Let's go in!" Tink exclaimed.

"Tinker Bell, we're not supposed to go near human houses!" cautioned Vidia.

"The sign says Fairies Welcome," countered Tink. She went inside and looked around, delighted by the tiny furnishings.

"Come on, Vidia," said Tink. "It's perfectly safe."

"Oh, really?" Vidia replied. She whipped up a gust of wind that slammed the door shut.

Tink didn't mind. She was having fun exploring the miniature house's gadgets.

But just then, Vidia saw a human approaching in the distance. She pulled on the door to let Tink out, but it was jammed shut!

Vidia hid, watching as Lizzy got closer. "Oh no! What have I done?" she cried as she watched Lizzy peer into the house.

"A...a...a fairy..." Lizzy whispered in astonishment.

Lizzy couldn't believe she had finally found a fairy! She knelt down to get a closer look. Then she picked up the fairy house with Tinker Bell inside and ran home!

Lizzy went upstairs to her room, placed the fairy house on the bed, and peeked in one of its windows. But Tinker Bell was nowhere to be seen.

"Where have you gone?" wondered Lizzy. She took the roof off the house and—ZIP!—Tink darted out.

Mr. Twitches immediately lunged for the fairy.

Vidia watched from the window, horrified, as Lizzy put Tinker Bell in a birdcage for safekeeping.

"Don't worry," the little girl told her. "Mr. Twitches won't bother you as long as you're in here." Then she picked up the menacing cat and carried him out of the room.

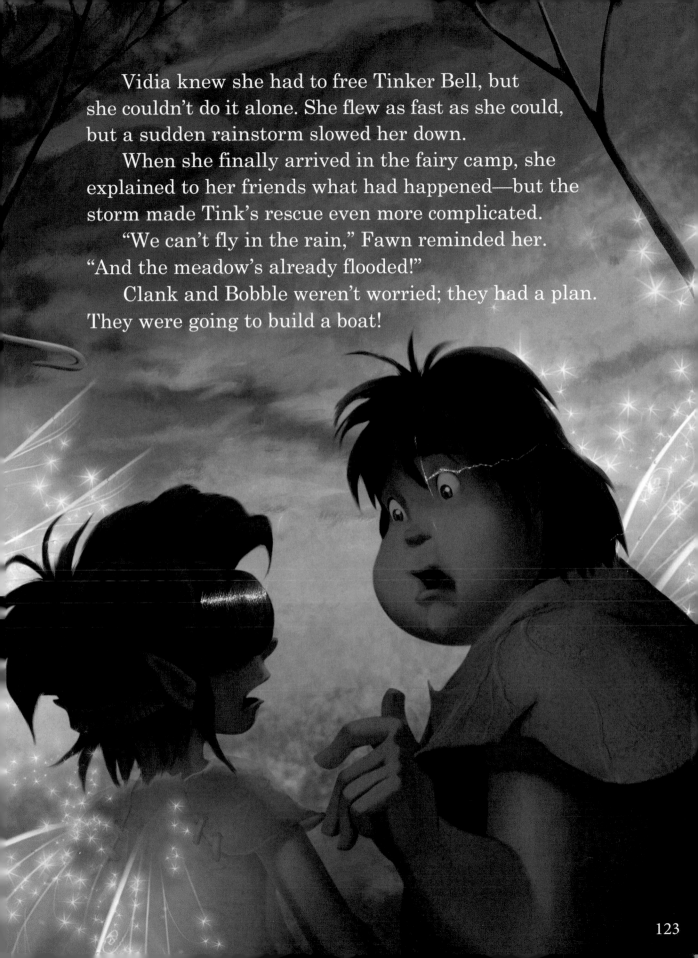

Vidia knew she had to free Tinker Bell, but she couldn't do it alone. She flew as fast as she could, but a sudden rainstorm slowed her down.

When she finally arrived in the fairy camp, she explained to her friends what had happened—but the storm made Tink's rescue even more complicated.

"We can't fly in the rain," Fawn reminded her. "And the meadow's already flooded!"

Clank and Bobble weren't worried; they had a plan. They were going to build a boat!

The entire camp set to work immediately.
Under Clank and Bobble's direction,
fairies and insects alike pitched in to create
a hull out of bark, a mast out of reeds and
twigs, and a sail out of a lily pad.

"It's working!" cried Clank as they put
all the parts together.

The fairy boat floated through the water smoothly, but out of nowhere the water became choppy. The rescuers were in a panic. They were headed for a waterfall!

"Hang on, we're going straight down!" yelled Bobble. Silvermist reached into the waterfall, making the water rise up so that the drop wasn't as steep. After a wild ride, the boat crashed onshore. The fairies lay scattered—but unharmed—around the wreckage.

"I guess our sailing days are over," said Bobble.

After getting up and making their way through the mud, the fairies paused in a meadow.

"I was just thinking of Tink," said Silvermist. "I really miss her."

"Listen," Vidia said. "Tinker Bell getting trapped is all my fault. I was trying to teach her a lesson, and I've put her and all of us in serious danger. I'm so sorry."

The fairies were very understanding.

They gathered around Vidia and chanted the fairy motto: "Faith, trust, and pixie dust!" Vidia loved feeling like part of the group.

Then they took off toward Lizzy's house.

"Okay," began Vidia. "Tinker Bell is upstairs. The little girl has her in a cage. There's also a large human who doesn't believe in fairies."

"Great!" Fawn exclaimed. "Anything else?"

But before Vidia could reply, the fairies had their answer.

Mr. Twitches was standing in the doorway!

He headed for the staircase and blocked the way. If the fairies wanted to get to Tinker Bell, they would have to get past him first.

Vidia had an idea. She shot a stream of pixie
dust at a plate, which began to hover in the air.
The others joined in, sprinkling the dust on dishes
and silverware. The fairies hurried across their
makeshift bridge to reach the stairs—but Mr.
Twitches was right behind them.

"You know where Tink is," Rosetta told Vidia.
"You go. We'll take care of the cat."

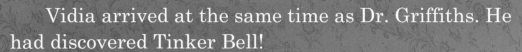

Vidia arrived at the same time as Dr. Griffiths. He had discovered Tinker Bell!

He stepped back in shock. "It can't be!" he cried.

"Isn't she wonderful?" asked Lizzy.

"Extraordinary," Dr. Griffiths agreed. "I'm very much intrigued by her. This is going to be the discovery of the century!"

Vidia watched as he raised a jar he had grabbed from one of Lizzy's shelves.

"Watch out!" she warned. She flew over and knocked Tink out of the way.

SLAM!

The jar came down and captured Vidia instead.

"I must get this to the museum right away!" declared Dr. Griffiths.

The fairies heard his footsteps approaching and quickly hid. But Lizzy's father was too excited about his new discovery to notice anything else.

"Please wait!" Lizzy begged, following him out into the rain. Lizzy was unable to stop her father. Tinker Bell watched nervously as Dr. Griffiths drove off toward the city.

Tinker Bell flew out of the room in a panic. She found her friends in the hallway and was very happy to see them.

But now it was her turn to try to save Vidia. She quickly told the fairy rescue team what happened to Vidia in the bedroom.

It was still raining, so Fawn asked, "How are we going to get there?"

137

"Maybe we can't fly," said Tinker Bell. "But I know someone who can."

Lizzy was nervous as the fairies bundled her up in a rain slicker and hat.

Tink looked at her friend as if to say "You can do it!"

"Okay. I'll be brave," Lizzy promised.

The fairies swirled around Lizzy and showered her with pixie dust.

"All aboard!" cried Tinker Bell.

Tink settled under Lizzy's collar, while the other fairies tucked themselves into her raincoat pockets.

Lizzy had a rough start, but soon she was maneuvering smoothly above the country road that led to the city.

Dr. Griffiths arrived at the museum, grabbed the jar with Vidia in it, and raced off toward the entrance.

Tinker Bell, Lizzy, and the fairies were right behind him.

"Father!" Lizzy called. Dr. Griffiths turned to see his daughter flying toward him, pixie dust trailing behind her.

Dr. Griffiths couldn't believe his eyes! "How are you doing that?" he asked. "There's no feasible scientific explanation. It has to be…magic."

Lizzy smiled. "It is," she told him.

"But where does it come from?" Dr. Griffiths wondered.

"Fairies," answered Lizzy matter-of-factly.

Suddenly, her father understood. "You're right," he agreed.

He handed the jar to Lizzy, and Vidia was reunited with her friends.

Then everyone—including Dr. Griffiths—headed back to the country, courtesy of a generous sprinkling of pixie dust.

The next day, the fairies and humans enjoyed a lovely tea party in the meadow together.

No one was more in the spirit of the carefree day than Dr. Griffiths.

"Isn't this pleasant, Father?" asked Lizzy.

"I can't imagine anything better," her father answered. "Although flying is a close second."

The End

Tinker Bell and the Secret of the Wings

Seasons come and seasons go, but in a magical place called Pixie Hollow, spring, summer, autumn, and winter exist side by side. The warm fairies live in spring, summer, and autumn. The winter fairies live in the snowy season of winter. No matter where they live, though, fairies always help one another.

In Tinkers' Nook, tinker fairies were making snowflake baskets for the fairies of winter while Fairy Mary supervised.

"I can't believe we make the baskets, but we don't get to take them to the winter fairies," Tinker Bell said to her friends Bobble and Clank.

"You'd get pounced on by a glacier!" Clank joked.

Just then, a group of snowy owls arrived and began to pick up the baskets. One owl brought Fairy Mary a note made of ice.

"They need twenty more baskets for tomorrow's pickup!" she announced.

Tink watched as the majestic birds headed off toward the Winter Woods. How she wished she could go with them!

153

A few minutes later, Tink ran into her friend Fawn.
"Look out!" Fawn cried suddenly as she chased a bunny
through the tinkers' workshop. Fawn needed to round up the
animals for their trip across the border to the Winter Woods.
Tink helped Fawn catch the bunny. "You're taking the
animals today?" she asked. "How about if I help?" This was
Tinker Bell's chance to see where the winter fairies lived!

Fawn agreed, and soon the two fairies were escorting the animals to the border that separated autumn from winter.

Fawn told Tink that only the animals were permitted to cross the border.

"No warm fairies are allowed in the Winter Woods, just like winter fairies aren't allowed over here."

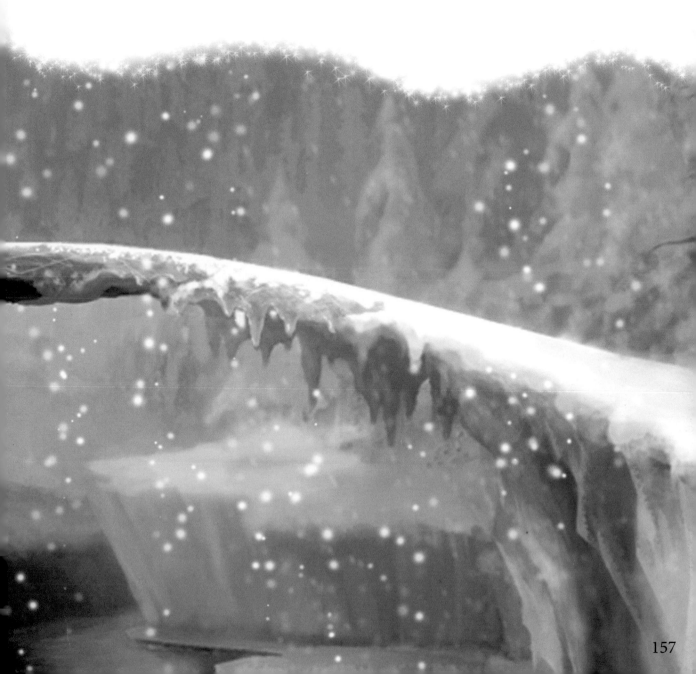

While Fawn was distracted, Tinker Bell moved closer to the border. The air was freezing!

She jumped in and looked around in wonder at the wintry landscape. She admired the sparkling snowflakes that drifted down from the sky.

Suddenly, her wings lit up in a beautiful burst of colorful light!

At that moment, Fawn yelled, "I told you we're not allowed to cross!"

Tinker Bell understood, but she wanted to know more. She was sure there was an explanation.

Tink headed to the Book Nook to do some research.
She grabbed a book and looked through it. But a
bookworm had chewed some of the pages, so she
wasn't able to understand anything!

A few minutes later, Tinker Bell spotted a wing-shaped book on one of the shelves. As she eagerly reached for it, the book flew away! She quickly chased after it. "Gotcha!" she cried.

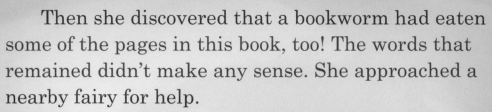

Then she discovered that a bookworm had eaten some of the pages in this book, too! The words that remained didn't make any sense. She approached a nearby fairy for help.

"Do you know anything about sparkling wings?" she asked.

"No, but the Keeper does," he replied. "He is the Keeper of All Fairy Knowledge. But he's a winter fairy. In order to talk to him, you have to go to the Winter Woods."

The next morning, Tink set off to find the Keeper. She put on a winter coat and tucked her wings inside to keep warm. Then she loaded the heavy book into her satchel.

Since Tink couldn't fly, she decided to travel to the Winter Woods by hiding in a snowflake basket!

With the help of a winter owl, Tink was
carried across the snowy valley. A winter animal
fairy named Sled appeared.

"You ready for the drop-off?" he asked the owl.

Tink quickly ducked down. The owl hooted
nervously, dived, and then let go of the basket.

Tink started falling fast!
"Look out!" cried the
Snowflake Fairies below.
Tinker Bell's basket
crashed and scattered
snowflakes everywhere.

Her book had been flung from the basket, too. Around the basket, she heard fairies talking. One was Lord Milori, the ruler of the Winter Woods.

While the fairies talked, Tink edged closer to her book and used her foot to try to grab it. But the book slid across the ice and landed right under Lord Milori's boot!

"Now, that is odd," he remarked. He picked it up and handed it to Sled.

"Return this to the Keeper," he said. "He can send it back to the warm side with his next delivery."

As Sled headed to see the Keeper, Tink secretly trailed behind him into the Hall of Winter. She waited until he had dropped off the book, and then slipped inside the icy hall.

As Tinker Bell made her way into the room, she spotted the Keeper sitting behind an easel.

She also noticed a shadow of a fairy—whose wings were sparkling!

Suddenly, Tink's wings began to sparkle, too!

Tinker Bell and the winter fairy, whose name was Periwinkle, flew around each other in awe. They didn't know what was happening!

The Keeper, Dewey,
couldn't believe his eyes.
"In all my years..." he
marveled. "Follow me."

Dewey guided them onto a giant snowflake. It lit up, and when Tink and Peri put their wings into a ribbon of light, the chamber filled with images! The fairies saw the journey of a baby's first laugh—a laugh that split in two!

One half of the laugh traveled to the Pixie Dust
Tree on the warm side—then Tinker Bell was born.

The other half blew into the Winter
Woods, where Periwinkle was born.

Tinker Bell and Periwinkle gasped. What did this mean?

Dewey had the answer. He explained that they were born of the same laugh.

"That is why your wings sparkle," said Dewey. "They're identical!"

"We're sisters!" Tinker Bell and Peri realized.

"You must have been at the border," Tink told Periwinkle.

"Yes," Peri replied. "I was hoping to see the animals cross."

The two fairies quickly discovered they had a
lot in common, especially their love of pom-poms!

Dewey told the girls they could spend some time together before Tink had to go home. The sisters were delighted!

Tink and Peri talked nonstop, trying to learn all about each other.

Peri showed Tinker Bell a bundle of items she had collected.

"I call them Found Things," Periwinkle said.

The sisters met up with Peri's friends
Gliss and Spike and went ice-sliding.
Tinker Bell had a wonderful time!

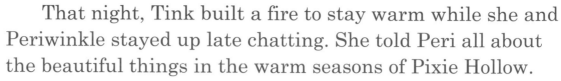

That night, Tink built a fire to stay warm while she and Periwinkle stayed up late chatting. She told Peri all about the beautiful things in the warm seasons of Pixie Hollow.

Periwinkle wished she could go there!

Tinker Bell and Peri decided this wasn't going to be the last time they would see each other.

Tink would find a way to tinker a machine that would allow Peri to come visit her in the warm seasons.

At that moment, Dewey and Fiona, a snowy lynx, arrived.

It was time for Tinker Bell to return home.

Lord Milori had decided that Tink crossing the border alone was too dangerous.

Tinker Bell and Peri gave each other a hug good-bye.

"I can't watch, Fiona!" Dewey cried.

Although Tinker Bell was sad, she left the Winter Woods with the best gift of all—a sister!

The End

Tinker Bell and the Pirate Fairy

It was another busy day for the fairies of Pixie Hollow. Everyone was heading to work, including an enthusiastic fairy named Zarina.

But while the other fairies flew to work, Zarina walked. This was strange because she was a dust-keeper fairy, and she worked with the golden pixie dust that helped fairies fly.

Zarina sprinted through the door of the Depot and took her place on the assembly line—the spot where all the golden pixie dust was packaged.

Zarina sprinkled some pixie dust on her hair to see what it would do—her hair stood straight up!

When Fairy Gary, the head dust-keeper, appeared, he announced that it was Zarina's turn for Blue Dust Duty.

Inside the Blue Pixie Dust Vault, Fairy Gary gave Zarina instructions for gathering the Blue Dust.

"Exactly twenty-six specks," he said.

"But why?" she asked.

"Zarina, you are the most inquisitive fairy I've ever known. Correction: It's a tie. Let's just say you are the Tinker Bell of dust-keepers."

Zarina smiled.

Once they collected the twenty-six specks, Zarina and Fairy Gary headed for the Pixie Dust Tree. Fairy Gary poured the Blue Dust into a container, and they watched as it dropped, one speck at a time, into the well of golden dust.

As the Blue Dust hit the golden dust, the golden dust flowed faster and grew brighter.

"Let me be absolutely clear, Zarina," Fairy Gary said. "Dust-keepers are forbidden to tamper with pixie dust."

Back at her cottage, Zarina emptied her daily allowance of pixie dust into a large jar. That was why she walked everywhere—she was saving all her dust for experiments!

So far, no matter what she tried, the golden pixie dust always stayed the same. With a sigh, she shut her experiment journal and laid her head down.

Suddenly, she noticed a dot of blue glowing on top of her journal. A speck of Blue Dust must have fallen from her hair!

Looking at the Blue Dust, Zarina felt inspired.

Delicately, she cut slivers from the speck.

Then she tried one of her experiments again—but this time, she added a speck of Blue Dust.

As she stirred, the golden dust suddenly turned orange! With her hand coated in the dust, Zarina found she could bend light.

Zarina was overjoyed. She couldn't wait to show Tinker Bell her discovery!

Tink was amazed when she saw the orange dust Zarina had created.

"That's never been done before," Tink said hesitantly.

"I'm doing more!" declared Zarina.

This time, the dust she created was purple, and with it, Zarina created a fast-flying whirlwind!

"Zarina, I really think you should stop!" Tink said firmly.

Surprised by Tink's yelling, Zarina accidentally spilled all the pink dust she had just created onto a potted plant.

Suddenly, thick vines rapidly grew, breaking out of the cottage.

The vines spread across Pixie Hollow, destroying everything—including the Dust Depot!

Queen Clarion was relieved to discover that no one was hurt. But when Fairy Gary saw the pink dust, he told Zarina that she would no longer be allowed to work as a dust-keeper fairy.

Zarina's eyes filled with tears. She loved pixie dust and being a dust-keeper.

She flew home and packed up her stockpile of dust.

After one last look around, she sprinkled dust on her wings and flew away from Pixie Hollow.

One year later, the fairies of Pixie Hollow were celebrating the Four Seasons Festival. But while all the fairies watched the show...

...someone snuck in and stole all the Blue Pixie Dust! Without the magic dust, the fairies wouldn't be able to make golden pixie dust, which meant they wouldn't be able to fly anymore.

Tinker Bell told the fairies that she saw Zarina during the show and wondered if she had taken the dust.

"What could she want it for?" asked Silvermist.

"I don't know, but we have to find her!" cried Tink.

Tinker Bell and her friends Vidia, Silvermist, Rosetta, Fawn, and Iridessa set off to follow Zarina. They knew they had to get the Blue Dust back.

The search party zoomed through the woods.

"There!" Iridessa cried. The glow from the Blue Dust was up ahead—and moving fast! It had to be Zarina!

The fairies flew higher as they neared the coast. They spotted a pirate ship!

And on its way to the pirate ship was a rowboat with a blue glow. They needed to get closer.

The girls flew down, taking care not to be spotted by the three pirates, and peered through a knothole.

Inside the boat, Zarina was holding up the Blue Pixie Dust triumphantly. The fairies couldn't believe what they were seeing.

"Let me just say your plan worked perfectly, Captain," said James, the cabin boy.

The other pirates bowed to their tiny leader—Zarina was now a pirate!

"Let's just get the dust and get out of here,"
ordered Tink.

The fairies sprang into action. Rosetta grew
seaweed that grabbed the oars.

Iridessa reflected a moonbeam into James's
eyes, and Silvermist rocked the boat with a wave.

When James fell,
Vidia snatched the
Blue Dust, tossed it
to Tink, and then
blocked Zarina
as she attempted
to follow.

The girls headed for the shore, but Zarina caught up quickly and demanded they return the dust.

Tink refused. "This dust belongs to Pixie Hollow," she said.

Zarina's eyes narrowed as she reached into her pocket. Suddenly, she hurled a fistful of pixie dust at the girls—but the dust was all different colors!

The dust knocked Tink and her friends backward through a waterfall. Zarina grabbed the bag of Blue Dust and quickly flew away.

As they stood up and shook themselves off, they realized that Zarina's dust switched their outfits—and their talents!

Now Tink was a water fairy! She tried to part a nearby waterfall but hit Vidia by accident. Fawn tried to control light, while Rosetta was covered in bugs! Eventually they were able to get used to their new talents.

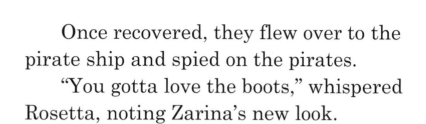

Once recovered, they flew over to the
pirate ship and spied on the pirates.

"You gotta love the boots," whispered
Rosetta, noting Zarina's new look.

"Shhhhh!" scolded Tink. She wanted to
hear what Zarina and the pirates were saying.

James was giving a toast to Zarina.

"Just one year ago, we'd lost everything…and then we found her." James nodded at Zarina. "We needed a captain. And when we humbly asked if she could make us fly…"

The fairies gasped at James's words. Zarina had become a pirate captain! Even more shocking, she planned to make the *whole pirate ship fly*!

The pirates cheered as the ship sailed toward a scary cave known as Skull Rock.

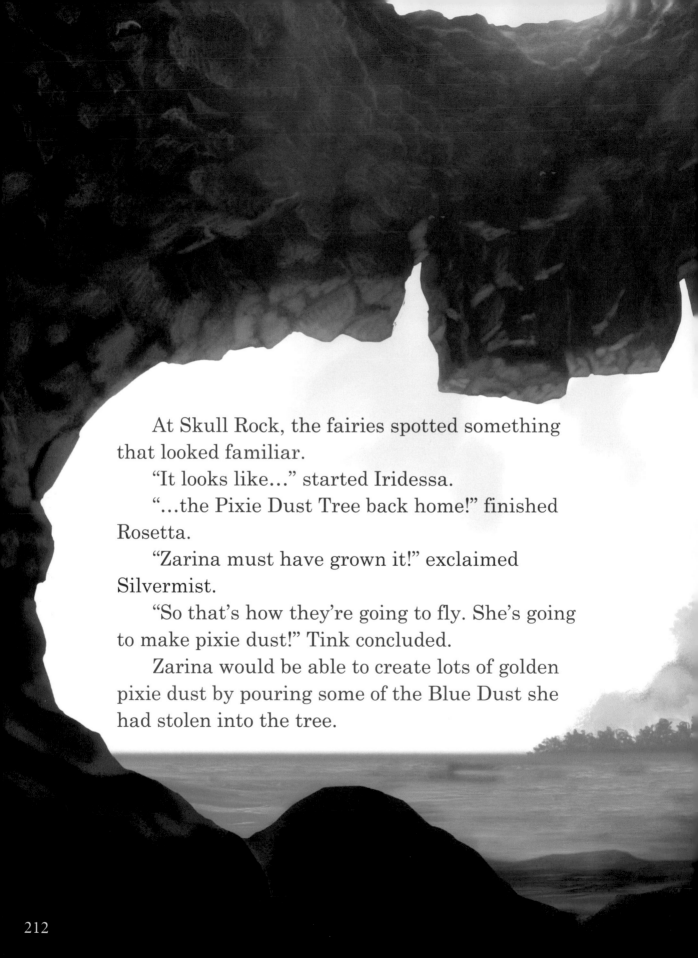

At Skull Rock, the fairies spotted something that looked familiar.

"It looks like…" started Iridessa.

"…the Pixie Dust Tree back home!" finished Rosetta.

"Zarina must have grown it!" exclaimed Silvermist.

"So that's how they're going to fly. She's going to make pixie dust!" Tink concluded.

Zarina would be able to create lots of golden pixie dust by pouring some of the Blue Dust she had stolen into the tree.

The fairies watched as Zarina carried the Blue Dust up
into the Pixie Dust Tree.

"Maybe we should try to talk to her," Tink replied.

"That didn't work at the waterfall," Vidia said in
disagreement.

A bee started to buzz around Iridessa. "Shoo!" she whispered.

As she tried to get away from the bee, Iridessa knocked into a branch. Her touch gave it a growth spurt! The branch shot out toward Zarina, taking all the girls with it!

Zarina quickly pointed her sword at the girls and whistled.

A pirate swooped in and nabbed the fairies with a fishing net.

Tinker Bell cried out, "Zarina, don't do this! Come back home!"

Zarina laughed. "I'll never go back to Pixie Hollow!" she vowed.

Meanwhile, Zarina opened the vial and let the Blue Dust flow into the tree. Everyone held their breath.

The tree glowed and shook and then…produced a tiny bit of golden pixie dust!

Zarina beamed with happiness!

Outside the ship, the golden pixie dust was flowing steadily. Zarina sprinkled some on James.

"I'm doing it! I'm flying!" James cried in excitement as he soared through the air.

After an exhilarating flight, James confirmed with Zarina that as long as they had Blue Dust, they would never run out of golden dust.

"Well then, we won't be needing you anymore," James announced with an evil grin. He grabbed the stunned Zarina and shut her inside a lantern!

"Our plan worked perfectly!" James added. "With a flying ship, there is no stopping us!"

He tossed Zarina and the lantern overboard. "Bon voyage, little captain!"

James had used Zarina for her talent. He was never really her friend.

Tink and the girls escaped the net and hurried off the ship. They saw the lantern with Zarina inside it! The lantern was starting to sink.

"Help me!" cried Zarina. The fairies zoomed over to rescue her.

"I'm so sorry," Zarina said.

Tinker Bell smiled warmly at her. The group of fairies forgave their old friend. Now it was time to stop those pirates!

As a team, they soared off in pursuit of the pirates.

Armed with tiny hatpins, the fairies were prepared to fight.

They demanded the pirates return the dust, but the pirates laughed at the tiny fairies. The pirates didn't believe they could be hurt by such small foes, but they were in for a big surprise!

"Our talents!" shouted Tinker Bell to her friends.
The girls worked together using their new talents
to stop the ship and knock the pirates overboard!

James sprinkled golden dust on himself and tried
to fly away. But Zarina saw one speck of Blue Dust
and hurled it at the pirate. The Blue Dust mixed with
the gold dust and multiplied it. James flew out of
control and right into a big wave of water.

"Can't fly when you're wet!" cried Zarina. "Good-
bye, James!"

The fairies had saved the day! They headed home to Pixie Hollow.

"Queen Clarion, we got the Blue Dust back!" cried Tinker Bell. "We also got Zarina!"

"Well then, the Blue Dust isn't the most valuable thing you brought back to me today," said the queen. She welcomed Zarina home and invited her to show off her new pixie dust alchemy talent.

Zarina smiled at her friends. She was happy to be home again.

The End

Tinker Bell and the Legend of the Never Beast

On a night like any other in Pixie Hollow, Iridessa, a light-talent fairy, gathered moonbeams. She didn't notice the mysterious green star in the sky—until it began to move. It was a comet!

The comet's light also drew the attention of
Tinker Bell, a tinker-talent fairy.

Scribble, a reading-talent sparrow man,
watched it through a telescope. He knew that the
last time the comet had appeared in Pixie Hollow
was almost one thousand years before.

The light from the comet continued on, brightening every dark corner and crevice. And as the light spilled deep down into a cave, something began to stir!

The next morning, Fawn, an animal-talent fairy, began her day as usual. She tumbled happily with the bugs, jumped with the bunnies...

...and soared through the
sky with the birds. Out of
all the animal fairies, Fawn
really embraced her job.

Later that day, Tink brought Fawn a handmade wagon. "Just like you ordered," said Tink. "But what are you up to?"

With a firm grasp on Tink's arm, Fawn warned, "Just try not to scream...deal?"

When Tink peeked into Fawn's home, two big eyes blinked open.

"Hawks eat fairies!" gasped Tink.

Fawn explained that Hannah was harmless. She had fixed the bird's wing, and it was time to let her go.

"We have to get Hannah out without causing widespread panic!" Fawn said.

Reluctantly, Tink helped put Hannah into the wagon and covered her with blueberries. But all the fairies and animals stared as they went by.

"What's with the berries?" asked Rosetta, a garden-talent fairy.

"Oh, we're just taking them to the forest," said Fawn.

But Rosetta knew how to move the berries faster.

With a sprinkle of pixie dust, the fruit rose—and uncovered Hannah, who screeched!

In the nearby forest, three adult hawks heard Hannah's cry and rushed to help her. The birds of prey swooped in, chasing after the fairies and threatening the animals in the nursery.

Fawn went after Hannah, while Tink led the other animals toward a hollow tree.

"Go!" she yelled. "Get inside!"

Iridessa flew away as fast as she possibly could, but something grabbed her!

It was Nyx, the leader of the scout fairies. Nyx guided Iridessa to a tree, then turned to face the hawks. As the protectors of Pixie Hollow, the scouts used ropes, spears, and their lightning speed to confuse the birds and chase them away.

Against Fawn's protests, the scouts tossed a net over Hannah.

"Is everyone all right?" asked Queen Clarion. It wasn't the first time that Fawn had nurtured a dangerous animal.

"You've always let your heart be your guide, but…"

"But I also need to listen with my head," said Fawn. "I promise I will next time."

Fawn released Hannah and watched her friend fly away.

Fawn started the next morning determined to be a model animal fairy as she greeted the bunnies: Calista, Nico, and Paige.

"Good morning, students. Let's see some hopping!"

Suddenly, a loud deep moan rippled through the forest.

"I should probably check that out," Fawn said.

Following a trail of broken branches, she spotted a patch of fur sticking out from beneath a rock. Just then, Fawn realized she was standing in a gigantic paw print!

Carefully, Fawn followed the paw prints and ended up outside a dark cave. She flew in and found a huge beast with glowing green eyes, a thick snout, and swirl-patterned gray fur.

"What are you?" she whispered.

Fawn tried to keep her cool when the enormous creature stood up. Without warning, the beast let out a ground-shaking "ROOOOAAARRRR!"

The roar was heard all across Pixie Hollow. It alarmed Nyx and the other scouts.

Fawn quickly flew out of the cave.

Fawn didn't get very far before she returned to the beast. She hid behind a rock until he emerged from his cave. When she flew in closer, she noticed a thorn stuck in his paw—she needed to help him. He was limping in pain!

Fawn watched from afar as the beast moved toward a big pile of rocks. He sorted through them, keeping only the red ones.

Fawn suspended one of the rocks from a tree. When the beast stood high on his hind legs to get the rock, she yanked the thorn from his paw.

The next day, Fawn began her study of the
strange creature. She drew him from every
angle, measured him, and tried to play with
him. She even dressed up like him.

But the animal
ignored her. All he
wanted to do was
build his rock pile.
So Fawn decided
to go to bed.

It was dawn when the big animal woke Fawn.

"Whoa, looks like somebody's a night owl!" she said as she studied the horn-shaped tower behind him.

Suddenly, the beast picked her up and plopped her on his head.

Together they marched into the forest.

"Where are we going?" asked Fawn.

The creature grumbled.

"Well, you don't have to be so gruff about it," she complained. Then it hit her. "That's what I'll call you—Gruff!"

Gruff stopped at a clearing in the Summer Forest. He dug out another boulder, and the process began again.

But Fawn turned it into a game. She sprinkled pixie dust on a boulder, and Gruff knocked it into place.

"Yes!" Fawn shouted, lining up a row of boulders. They were having such a fun time together!

Fawn decided to introduce Gruff to Tink and the fairies. "I'm sure you're wondering what this is about," Fawn said. She took a deep breath. "Ladies, say hello to Gruff."

Gruff swung down from the tree, hanging upside down by his tail.

The fairies gasped, and Iridessa fainted.

"What is that?" gulped Rosetta.

Fawn explained how she met Gruff and how other fairies in Pixie Hollow think Gruff is a monster called the NeverBeast.

"I know he's not what they say he is," Fawn said. Fawn believed he was there to save the day.

In the morning, thick green clouds covered the sky. The girls watched in wonder as lightning began to strike and huge wings grew from Gruff's back. He had grown horns, too! They understood his purpose now.

"The towers—they draw lightning so he can collect it," Fawn said. "It's what he's been preparing for the whole time!

We're going to the towers. Okay, big guy. Just follow my glow!"

257

Fawn led Gruff to the Autumn Tower, which glowed from a constant stream of lightning hits. Gruff charged at it, and the lightning jumped to his horns. Then the tower crumbled, and the lightning cleared from the area.

Fairies on the ground watched in amazement as Fawn led Gruff overhead.

At the Winter Tower, Gruff twisted and turned as he again absorbed the lightning.

"One more to go!" shouted Fawn.

As Fawn and
Gruff reached
the final tower,
Gruff struck it,
which caused
it to open and
scatter lightning
everywhere!

Gruff stepped in and absorbed all the lightning. In one gigantic blast, Gruff shook off the energy waves, sending them far out over the sea. The storm was over!

Gruff's fur was burned and his horns were broken. He was weak from absorbing all the lightning.

Gruff lowered himself next to Fawn and nudged her with his nose. Fawn nuzzled him back.

"That's my big furry monster!" she shouted.

The fairies cheered. Gruff had protected the fairies and saved Pixie Hollow from the storm!

Before long, Gruff
made a full recovery.
Gruff was a hero to
the fairies.

Gruff helped repair the damage from the storm. But soon he started to tire. Fawn listened to his heartbeat and knew it was time for him to go back into hibernation.

"How long are we talking about?" asked Rosetta.

Fawn held back her tears. "About a thousand years."

The girls understood what that meant. "We'll never see him again," said Tink.

Fawn and the girls led Gruff back to his cave. Hundreds of fairies lined the route to wish him well.

Inside the cave, Tink had made him a special bed. Rosetta had given him a fluffy pillow. Silvermist had put in a spring-fed water bowl. Iridessa had brought a night-light. And Vidia had added a gentle breeze.

Nyx gave Gruff something, too. "The enduring respect of a grateful scout."

"Hey, big guy," Fawn said. "I won't see you again. But I know you'll always be there when we need you." Gruff settled into his bed and smiled. Fawn kissed him on the nose. "I'm really going to miss you," she whispered as he fell asleep. "I love you, Gruff."

The End